$14.95 BiT 10/02   E

Signs
of
Spring

by Justine Korman Fontes
Illustrated by Rob Hefferan

For Kathy, Robbie, Allison,
and all our friends in Maine
who truly appreciate
the first signs of spring!
—J.K.F.

For information contact:
MONDO Publishing
980 Avenue of the Americas
New York, NY 10018

Visit our web site at http://www.mondopub.com

Printed in the United States of America

02 03 04 05 06 07 HC 9 8 7 6 5 4 3 2 1
02 03 04 05 06 07 PB 9 8 7 6 5 4 3 2 1

ISBN 1-59034-189-9 (hardcover)
ISBN 1-59034-180-5 (pbk.)

Designed by John Grandits

Library of Congress Cataloging-in-Publication Data

Korman, Justine.
    Signs of spring / by Justine Korman Fontes; illustrated by Rob Hefferan.
      p. cm.
    Summary: On the way to school one day Lucy and her two friends find many signs of
spring, from buds on trees to blades of grass.
    ISBN 1-59034-180-5 (pbk.) -- ISBN 1-59034-189-9
    [1. Spring--Fiction. 2. Show-and-tell presentations--Fiction. 3. Schools--Fiction. 4.
Mice--Fiction.] I. Hefferan, Rob, ill. II. Title.

PZ7.K83692 Si 2002
[E]--dc21
                                                                        2001055817

Every morning Lucy walked to school
with her best friends Henry and Zack.

But this brisk spring morning was different.
Lucy felt even bouncier than usual!

"Wait up!" Henry called.
He was out of breath.

Zack said, "Hurry up! Lucy doesn't
know how to wait."

"Can't you smell it?" Lucy squeaked.
"Spring is in the air!"

Zack sniffed the wind. But all
he got was a nose full of cold.

Henry sniffed, but all he got
was a nose full of fur!

A little further down the road, Lucy cried,
"Look! There are buds on the trees."

Lucy found a brand-new fern, still curled up tight.

She tucked it in her pocket.

All the way to school, Lucy collected
more signs of spring.

She picked up a robin's feather.

Lucy squeaked, "I can fly!"

"No, you can't but . . . you sure can run fast!"
Henry complained.

Lucy picked a daisy.

She tickled her chin with the soft flower.

Lucy plucked a blade of bright, green grass.

Then she found some moss.

"The first crocus!" Lucy called.
"Isn't it pretty?"

"Not as pretty as you, Lucy," Zack thought.
But he didn't say anything.

When the friends got to school,
Lucy's pockets were full.

In their classroom, their teacher, Miss Whiskers, was setting up for show-and-tell.

"What did you bring for show-and-tell, Lucy?" asked Henry.

Lucy gasped. "Oh, no! I forgot all about show-and-tell!"

"Please don't call on me! Please don't call on me!" Lucy whispered to herself.

But the teacher looked right at her.
"Lucy, will you go first?" she asked.

Lucy said softly, "Um . . . I forgot to
bring something."

Henry cleared his throat. He pointed
to Lucy's pockets.

Zack said, "You brought plenty
of somethings."

Lucy reached in her pockets. She smiled.

"I did find some signs of spring on the way to school," she said.

Lucy showed the class
her treasures, except for
the crocus. She gave that
to Miss Whiskers.

The teacher smiled.

"Lucy! That's the best springtime
show-and-tell I ever saw," said
Miss Whiskers.

Lucy grinned and said, "I couldn't have done it without my friends."

Lucy added, "I might forget show-and-tell, but I could never forget Henry and Zack."